P9-EKI-760

Frightfully Friendly Ghosties

Phantom Pirates

Also by Daren King

MOUSE NOSES ON TOAST

*SENSIBLE HARE AND
THE CASE OF CARROTS*

PETER THE PENGUIN PIONEER

The Frightfully Friendly Ghosties Series:

FRIGHTFULLY FRIENDLY GHOSTIES

GHOSTLY HOLLER-DAY

SCHOOL OF MEANIES

FRIGHTFULLY FRIENDLY GHOSTIES

Phantom Pirates

Quercus

Nestlé Gold Award Winner

DAREN KING

Quercus

New York • London

Text © 2012 by Daren King
Illustrations © 2012 by David Roberts
First published in the United States by Quercus in 2014

ISBN 978-1-62365-811-3

Library of Congress Control Number: 2014931816

Distributed in the United States and Canada by
Hachette Book Group
237 Park Avenue
New York, NY 10017

Manufactured in the United States

2 4 6 8 10 9 7 5 3 1

www.quercus.com

For Rebecca

Contents

1

The Competition

If you had seen us ghosties wafting by the water's edge that morning, laughing and singing summer songs, you may have thought we were headed somewhere pleasant.

How wrong you would be to think that!

I'm Pamela, by the way. Pamela Fraidy. Not that I'm afraid or anything.

It began two weeks earlier, the day the post-phantom delivered the letter—

No, that isn't right. It began two months before that, when Tabitha had one of her bright ideas, and every lightbulb in the house went *POP!*

I expect you know that Tabitha Tumbly is a poltergeist, the sort of ghosty who can make odd things happen just by thinking.

It's funny, but some ghosties find this frightening.

"Wither," Agatha said, "do light that candle, before we all bump into one another in the dark."

"Consider it lit," Wither said, and I heard that rough zipping sound a match makes as it strikes the side of a matchbox.

"That's better," Agatha said. "I say, where's Pamela?"

"I'm here," I said. "When the bulbs popped, I suddenly remembered I had to tidy up behind the bookcase."

"Do come out, Pamela," Tabitha said. "I want all six of us together, so I can tell you my idea."

And out I wisped.

"Let's hear it then," Wither said, and he rolled

his eyes and folded his bony arms.

"What us ghosties need," Tabitha said, "is a holler-day."

"Our last holler-day was a disaster," Agatha said.

Charlie straightened his fedora. "At Frighten-on-Sea? Yes, we spent most of the holler-day flecing that caped figure."

"And such rotten weather," Humphrey said, biting into a sausage roll.

"That," Wither said, "is why we need another holler-day. Is that what you were about to say, Tabitha?"

"Precisely," Tabitha said. "But this year, we holler-day in the June sunshine."

"We don't have time to organize a holler-day," Agatha said. "Charlie has twelve gold watches to sell, Humphrey has his schoolwork, Wither is elbow deep in unfinished poems, and you, Tabitha, have cupcake class. Oh, and I promised

3

I'd help my friend Eleanor pen her gothic novel."

"Pamela can organize the holler-day," Charlie said, and that was that.

On the first day of June, Tabitha wisped us all into the living room, declaring that today was the day I'd reveal our holler-day plan.

I was about to explain that the plan had fallen flat, when we heard a whistling sound from the front lawn.

"That post-phantom always whistles a cheerful tune," Wither said.

"Well," Charlie said, doffing his fedora, "it is the polite thing to do." And he passed through the wall to the hall.

You probably know that Charlie Vapor is the only ghosty who could do so. The rest of us have to use the door, like you still-alives.

Agatha prodded me on the arm. "Pamela, you were saying?"

"Yes," I said. "You see, I was about to order the holler-day brochure when I spotted a competition in the *Daily Wail*." I pulled a newspaper clipping from my pocket and held it up for all to see.

COMPETITION, it said in bold letters. WIN A SPECTRAL SUMMER CRUISE.

"The chances of winning a competition are one in a million," Humphrey groaned.

"I hadn't thought of that," I fibbed, and I was about to explain how we'd just have to spend summer in the safety of our own haunted home when Charlie passed back through the wall.

"How exciting!" Charlie said. "This letter is from that ghostly newspaper the *Daily Wail*. We've won a summer holler-day, on a still-alive ocean liner."

"Hoorah for Pamela Fraidy!" Agatha cried, clapping her hands.

"Pamela," Tabitha said, "you've turned white as a sheet."

6

The truth is, the thought of another ghostly holler-day terrified me. What if we got into frightful trouble or lost our way and couldn't get home?

"Um, it's the excitement," I said, and I wisped behind the bookcase to finish the tidying up.

2

Eleanor Wraith

The evening before the first day of the cruise, the six of us stayed at a ghostly guest house overlooking the harbor.

We did ask for a room in a still-alive guesthouse, but the still-alives yelled mean things and hid behind the counter.

"I'm sorry to be the bearer of bad news," I said as we floated down the shimmering corridor, "but I'm afraid we won't be setting sail after all."

"Why ever not?" Charlie said, jangling the brass room key.

"The cruise is for seven, and there are only six of us." I held up the newspaper clipping.

"Pamela," Tabitha said, "why didn't you mention this before we packed our suitcases?"

"We could've invited one of the other ghosties," said Humphrey Bump, bumping my case.

"Rusty Chains," Charlie suggested, "or Headless Leslie or Gertrude Goo."

"I didn't think about it," I said, biting my tongue.

"Fortunately," Agatha said, "I read the newspaper clipping myself, and I invited a friend. She's meeting us at the harbor before we board."

"Pamela," Tabitha said, "I'm starting to think you don't want to go on this summer cruise."

"She's a scaredy-cat," Humphrey said, and he bumped open the bedroom door and rolled into the room.

Early the next morning, as we wafted down to the harbor, we were greeted by the palest ghosty

I have ever laid eyes on. She was tall and willowy, like, um, a willow tree.

"This," Agatha said, "is my dear friend Eleanor Wraith."

"How lovely to meet you," Tabitha said, and four frightfully friendly ghosties shook Eleanor's ivory hand.

"Right," Wither said. "Now we can board the *Porcelain Princess* and begin our summer holler-day."

"And what a fine vessel she is," Charlie said, doffing his hat at the vast ocean liner.

"Wait," Eleanor said. "This Wither chap said there are seven of us, but I shook only four haunted hands."

"You didn't shake Agatha's hand," Tabitha said. "If you had shaken Agatha's hand, that would be five."

"Plus yourself," said Humphrey. "Five and one is seven. It's math."

"Five plus one equals six," corrected Wither.

"But Eleanor has two hands," Agatha said. "And five plus two equals seven."

Wither withered. "That's hardly the point."

"One of us is missing," Tabitha said. "And no prizes for guessing who."

"Pamela the scaredy-cat," Humphrey said. "We'd better find her. The ship is about to set sail."

The ghosties spent the next five minutes floating up and down the harbor, checking behind bollards and beneath the wings of seagulls, but the missing ghosty—that's me, by the way—was nowhere to be found.

"Are you looking for someone?" I said, and I wisped out from my hiding place inside Eleanor's felt hat.

Wither frowned. "Bother. And now our ship has sailed."

"Pamela!" Tabitha snapped. "You did that on purpose. You hid so that we would miss the boat."

"Tabitha, don't be mean," Wither said.

"I'm afraid Tabitha is right," I said, peering through my summer shoes. "Our holler-day is ruined, and it is my fault."

Wither cracked his knuckles. "Then it is you, Pamela, who is mean. Though I have to say, Tabitha is mean, too, for snapping at poor Pammy."

"Pamela," Tabitha said, "I'm sorry I snapped. But why did you make us miss the cruise?"

"I'm . . . I'm frightened of water," I said, and I hid my eyes with my hands.

"You're frightened of your own shadow," Wither said, and he gazed poetically out to sea, at the ocean liner sailing toward the glimmering horizon.

3

Stowaways!

"All is not lost," Agatha said after a moment's thought. "There is a way we can board the ocean liner after all."

"Oh yes?" said Wither, brightening.

"It says in the newspaper article that the ocean liner spends the first night at the Isle of Fright."

"Is the Isle of Fright terribly far?" I said.

"Barely an hour's waft," said Eleanor. "I visited the island while researching for my first novel, *The Pendulum Doth Swing*."

"Oh, what a lovely title!" Wither said, and his

13

eyes glazed.

"We'll hitch a ride on one of these dear little fishing boats," said Agatha. "I say!" she called out. "Can you help us?"

When the fishermen saw Agatha rattling her pearls, hair billowing in the breeze, they yelled mean things and covered their heads with their fishing nets.

"I expect they've got sunstroke," said Agatha, gazing up at the blue sky.

The farther along the harbor we floated, the meaner the still-alives became, and it wasn't long before we ran out of boats.

"Oh well," I said, clutching my suitcase to my chest. "We'll just have to catch the train home."

"There's a ship at the end of that jetty," Tabitha said, pointing at a wooden pathway that led out to sea.

The ship was called the *Raggy Dolly*, and it

looked about ready to set sail. It also looked ready to fall apart. The wooden sides stank of plankton and rot, and the sails were so worn they could barely waft.

"Now we're here," Eleanor said as we reached the end of the jetty, "we might as well have a nose around." And she floated aboard.

Agatha, Tabitha, Charlie, Wither, and Humphrey followed, leaving the suitcases in a heap.

I was trying to decide which frightened me more, the vast ocean or the journey home alone, when Tabitha grabbed my haunted hand and wisped me over the short stretch of water.

"Ahoy there!" Agatha called breezily, but no reply came.

After a minute of peering into barrels and behind sails, we stopped, and Charlie adjusted his fedora and turned to face the shore.

Then he froze.

"Charlie," Tabitha said, "whatever is the matter?"

"Wasn't the ship a little closer to our luggage?"

We wisped toward the rail at the rear of the ship.

Charlie was right. When we wafted aboard, the gap between ship and jetty had been a mere flit. Now it looked like a float and a half at least.

"I don't think we should risk it," Tabitha said. "We've never floated across open water before. I'm worried we might fall in."

The seven of us wisped this way and that—"henceforth and therefore," as Wither put it, the dear old fool—until Agatha rattled her pearls and declared that we were stowaways.

We floated around for a bit, then Wither said, "So we're stowaways then?"

"Stowaways," Agatha said.

"We're stowaways!" Wither cried, his poetry

voice wafting out across the open water.

"Stowaways we may be," Eleanor said, scribbling in her notepad, "but at least we're headed in the right direction." She unfolded a flute-like finger and pointed at a swelling shape on the horizon.

"The Isle of Fright," Charlie said. "We can board the ocean liner and begin our summer cruise."

But as the ship sailed on, the Isle of Fright drifted away to the left.

"How odd," said Wither. "The island is moving."

"The island isn't moving," Humphrey said, bumping Wither's bony elbow. "We've changed direction."

"Then I daresay we're sailing around the Isle of Fright and heading directly for France."

"Um," I said, hiding my eyes, "does anyone know how to steer a ship?"

4

Skull and Crossbones

As the Isle of Fright faded into the distance, the sky clouded over and a mist descended.

"I say," said Agatha, folding her arms, "what happened to the summer weather?"

"This does not bode well," said Wither.

"No," said Eleanor, scrawling in her notepad, "but it's frightfully inspiring."

"I'm tired, cold, and hungry," I said.

Humphrey shrugged. "I've got doughnuts in my suitcase."

"There's warm clothes in our cases too,"

Charlie said, buttoning his jacket. "Fat lot of good that is, with our luggage on the jetty."

"Let's huddle together, for warmth," Tabitha said. "If we float above the lookout platform at the front, we can keep an eye out for land."

"The front of a ship is known as the bow," Wither said as we wafted up the three rickety steps to the platform. "The sides are the portside and the starboard, and the back—"

"Shh," I said. "I heard something."

"That was my tummy rumbling," said Humphrey.

"Not that. It came from below deck, and it sounded like a door creaking open."

We listened.

CREEEEAAAAK!

"What was that?" Agatha said.

"The door again," I said, "creaking closed."

"Impossible," Charlie said. "We're alone."

A wooden hatch opened at the foot of the three rickety steps, and a figure emerged.

"It must be the still-alive who owns the ship," Tabitha said.

The mysterious figure closed the hatch and knelt by a coil of rope.

"Whoever they are," Charlie said, "they don't seem to know we're here. In this mist, us ghosties are almost invisible."

"I felt a spot of rain," said Wither. "Perhaps they'll allow us to shelter below deck."

"We'd better make friends with them," Agatha said. "Charlie, you're the polite one. Show us how it's done."

"Um, ladies first," Charlie said, hiding behind his hat.

"After you, Charlie Vapor," Tabitha said.

"I suppose it's up to me," said Agatha, but just as she was about to wisp down and greet the mysterious stranger, the sea breeze tore Charlie's hat from his head and tossed it onto the deck.

"Agatha, you did that with your powers, so I'd have to float down and fetch it."

I expect you know that Agatha Draft is the sort of ghosty who can create an eerie breeze.

"I suggest we all float down together," Tabitha said. "There's safety in numbers. Isn't that right, Wither?"

Wither nodded. "It's elementary mathematics."

The seven of us joined hands and floated down the steps, to where the mysterious figure knelt by a flagpole.

"There's something odd about that still-alive," Eleanor said, glancing at his wobbly, wafty legs.

"Eleanor, you're right," Tabitha said. "That isn't a still-alive. That's a ghosty."

"Thank heavens!" wailed Wither. "If they're

ghosties like us, they won't be mean."

"Pamela," Tabitha said, "tap him on the shoulder, let him know we're friends."

"We're, um, frightfully friendly," I said, but as I reached out a trembling hand the ghosty turned, baring two rows of blackened teeth.

A shiver ran down my spine, then walked back up it again.

"What an unsightly ghosty," Agatha said as we all wisped down to the rear of the ship. "The hollow cheekbones! Those crazy, staring eyes!"

"He looked like Wither," Humphrey said.

"I don't know about that," Tabitha said, "but I have to say, I didn't like the look of him one bit."

"Did you see how he's dressed?" Eleanor said. "Hoop earrings, fancy waistcoat   "

"What's he up to?" I said, covering my eyes.

"He's hoisting a ghostly flag," Eleanor said.

We huddled in fear as the black-toothed ghosty tugged at a rope. The phantom flag unfurled as it reached the top of the flagpole.

"What an odd flag," said Wither. "It's black, with a white skull, and two bones crossed over."

"A skull and crossbones," Agatha said with a gulp. "You know what that means."

"Erm," said Wither, cowering behind Humphrey's tummy. "That the bones are cross?"

"I'm afraid it's worse than that," I said. "The *Raggy Dolly* has been hijacked by phantom pirates."

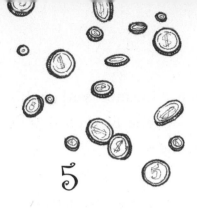

5

Gold Coins

The skies opened, and the rain came down in sheets.

"I think we should confront them," said Eleanor Wraith. "A swashbuckling adventure on the high seas! What could be more romantic?"

"Eleanor," Wither said, "this isn't a storybook. Our very lives are at stake. Well, not our lives—"

"Precisely," said Eleanor, and off she wisped.

"I guess we have no choice," Humphrey said, and we floated after Agatha's friend.

"Hello," Eleanor said, bobbing behind the ghosty with the blackened teeth. "We boarded this ship by mistake—"

"Unwittingly," added Wither.

"Not meaning any harm, if you catch my drift," Charlie said, and his hand trembled as he doffed a shaky fedora.

The phantom pirate bared his horrible teeth, and all seven of us floated back with a start. "Mistake or not, stowaways is stowaways, and on this ship you pays your way."

"We don't have any money," said Humphrey, and he turned out his pockets.

"Then you must work for your passage," the pirate growled.

"I refuse to lift a finger," Wither said, and he folded his flagpole arms.

A bolt of lightning tore across the rainy sky, and we almost leapt out of our spooky skins.

The pirate opened the wooden hatch, and out wisped two dozen of the fiercest, ugliest, meanest phantom pirates you have ever seen.

"Having said that," gulped Wither, "I don't mind a spot of light dusting."

Each pirate wore a fancy pirate outfit. Brightly colored puffy shirt, striped stockings, headscarves, leather boots, that sort of thing. Some had tattoos, others wore jewelry—stolen jewelry, I have no doubt.

"I love pirates!" Humphrey said, though I could tell he felt afraid.

The phantom pirates led us below deck, where a pirate with seaweed-colored eyes knocked on a door with a transparent hook hand. "Cap'n Mean-Beard, sir?"

"Enter if you're fool enough!" a voice boomed as the door creaked open on rusty hinges.

The Captain was a ghosty about the size of a

large wardrobe, with a thundery black beard, a ship-shaped hat and an eye patch on each eye. Behind one ear he carried a golden telescope.

"What do we have 'ere then?" the Captain yelled, rising from his ghostly chair.

"Stowaways," growled a pirate with a wooden leg. "We thought you might have use for 'em."

"I 'ave use for 'em all right," the Captain said, ruffling his beard. "They can count these pieces of eight." He emptied two sacks of ghostly coins onto the transparent table and floated out of the room.

"And we'll be checking your pockets when you're done," the hook-handed pirate scowled, and he slammed the door, causing the cabin to shake.

For the next hour, rain lashed against the portholes and the ship rocked this way and that as we counted the ghostly booty.

The moment Wither stacked the final coin,

Humphrey gave the table a bump, and two thousand coins clattered onto the floorboards.

"Sorry," Humphrey said. "I always bump tables when I'm spooked, and those pirates give me the willies."

The door burst open, and in wisped Captain Mean-Beard and the ghosty with the blackened teeth.

"I don't think counting coins is our area of expertise," Wither gulped. "Perhaps we could pen you a sea shanty?"

"Please understand," Charlie said, dropping his fedora, "we've never been in the company of pirates before, and—"

"We're too nervous to count coins," I said, hiding under the table.

"No matter," the Captain boomed, peering out from beneath one of his eye patches. "Now that the storm has passed, we've a bigger job for you." He turned to the ghosty with the blackened teeth. "Tooth Rot," he said, "show our prisoners the bristly broom."

"Arrr the bristly broom!" Tooth Rot sniggered.

"When they've swept the puddles," Captain Mean-Beard said, "lock 'em in a trunk."

"I don't like the sound of that," Wither crooned.

"And if they don't work hard enough," the Captain went on, "leave 'em on a desert island. A small one, with one palm tree and an angry baboon. We've important business to attend to, and we don't want no landlubbers gettin' in the way."

"Important business?" Tabitha whispered nervously. "What could he mean?"

"Those pirates are up to something," Charlie whispered, biting his lip. "And I'd bet it's as mean as Wither's poems are long."

6

Swept Deck

Tooth Rot led us back up to the top deck, where the peg-legged ghosty stood propped against a ghostly broom.

"You knows what that is, me hearty?" Tooth Rot said, and he prodded poor Wither in the ribs.

"A ghostly bristly broom," Wither said.

Tooth Rot pointed toward the ship's starboard side, where the hook-handed pirate floated above a puddle of rainwater. "And I daresay you knows what that is too."

Wither hid behind his trembling elbows. "Um, a puddle?"

"So, now you knows what your job is," Tooth Rot said. "And when that puddle is swept, there's plenty more just like it."

"If we had a broom each," Tabitha explained nervously, "we could sweep the puddles more quickly."

"One bristly broom is all we got," Tooth Rot said. "You'll have to take turns." And he wisped off below deck, the other phantom pirates wafting behind.

We each took a turn with the bristly broom, sploshing the water under the rail and over the side of the ship.

The problem was, the next puddle was twice the size, and the third bigger still. In the fourth, Tabitha found an octopus and six slippery fish.

"This is taking too long," said Humphrey Bump,

"and those fish make me want to eat chips."

"My arms hurt," said Tabitha. "Eleanor, it's your turn with the broom. Um, Eleanor, what are you writing?"

"Notes for my novel," Eleanor said, peering up from her notepad. "See how the breeze caresses the surface of the water?"

"How can you think about literature at a time like this?" Agatha asked.

"It takes my mind off the stomach-churning fear," Eleanor said.

"Wait," Tabitha said. "The rippling puddles have given me an idea. Agatha could create a breeze and blow the rainwater overboard."

"If only I had the skills," said Agatha, and she blushed bright white.

"Aggie," Eleanor said, "with skills like yours, you could blow the roof from a thatched cottage."

Agatha laughed. "My dear, I doubt I could ruffle the fur of a baby field mouse."

"We're in terrible danger," Charlie said. "If we don't act fast, those pirates will lock us in a trunk."

"Or leave us on a desert island," Humphrey said.

"A small one," Wither blubbed, "with one palm tree and an angry baboon."

"Oh, do try to blow the puddles, Aggie," Tabitha said.

Agatha tried.

At first, the puddles merely rippled. Then Agatha took a deep breath, and blew so hard that the water sprayed into the air and over the rail, where it cascaded into the sea.

"Did you ghosties see that?" Charlie asked excitedly.

"Explain," Tabitha said.

"When Agatha blew, the sails wafted," Charlie said. "A big puff would blow the *Raggy Dolly* all the way home."

"If I had the skills—"

"Agatha," Eleanor said, "we've had quite enough false modesty for one day."

"Close your eyes, then," Agatha said.

The six of us closed our eyes. At least, we pretended to.

Agatha huffed and puffed with all her might, and the ship turned and set sail for England.

"Bravo!" we cried, clapping our haunted hands.

"Shh, or the pirates will hear," Agatha said between puffs.

Too late. The hatch opened with an angry *THUD,* and out wafted the twenty-five ghostly crew members, followed by Mean-Beard, the ship's mean-spirited Captain.

In a panic, the pirates drew their cutlasses and slashed the ship's sails.

Agatha blew harder than ever, but it was no use. The eerie breeze passed right through.

"That's torn it," Wither said, and he blubbed.

7

Sewn Sails

"You'll pay for this!" the Captain boomed. "The *Raggy Dolly* is my ship, and I expects it to be shipshape."

"Repair the Captain's sails," growled the hook-handed pirate, "or we'll lock you in that trunk."

"With smelly pirate socks!" Tooth Rot added.

"Either that or we leave you on a desert island," the Captain said with a hearty laugh.

"A small one," Tooth Rot said, "with one palm tree and an angry baboon."

"If you can forgive me for saying," Tabitha said

nervously, "it wasn't us who slashed the sails."

Charlie took a watch from his jacket and offered it to the crew of phantom pirates. "Solid gold. Here, it's yours."

Tooth Rot grabbed the gold watch from Charlie's hand and bit it. "Tooth marks," he said, and tossed the watch overboard.

"So," the Captain growled, "first you ruin my ship's sails, then you try an' fool me with a fake gold watch." And he led his crew back down the hatch.

A minute later, the hook-handed pirate floated back up, a pouch swinging from his hook. "You knows what this is?" he growled, his seaweed-colored eyes glinting menacingly.

"It looks like a knitting bag or purse," Wither said, and he pursed his lips and knitted his brow.

"This," the pirate said, "is a sewing kit. And that, behind me, is a slashed sail. When that sail's sewn, there's plenty more jus' like it."

"There's only one needle," Wither said, peering into the pouch.

"One needle is all we got," the pirate snapped. "You'll 'ave to take turns." He wisped below deck, closing the wooden hatch behind him.

"Wither is the only ghosty who can sew," Agatha said. "Well, I can sew, but not with cold fingers."

"My fingers are cold too, Aggie," Wither said.

"Oh, don't make such a fuss!" Agatha said.

Wither took out a spool and bit off a length of thread. He floated halfway up the sail and set to work.

The problem was, Wither can only sew while reciting poetry, and Wither's poems are drivel.

"At this rate, we'll be here all night," Eleanor said with her fingers in her ears.

"We'd better think of something quick,"

Humphrey said, "before the pirates come back with that trunk of smelly pirate socks."

"If only we had more needles," Tabitha sighed.

"I have twelve sewing needles right here," Eleanor said, and she tugged a tiny tin from her pocket. "But what good are they when only one ghosty can sew?"

I saw the look in Tabitha's eye, and I guessed what she was thinking.

"Eleanor," I said, "hand those needles to Tabitha. Wither, we'll need your help."

"I didn't know you could sew, dearest

Tabitha," Wither wailed in his poetry voice, and he floated down from the sail.

"Wither, I can't sew to save my life. Um, not that I'm alive. But if the spirits are with us, the sails will sew themselves."

We watched excitedly as Wither threaded each needle and passed it to Tabitha, who placed all thirteen needles in a row at the foot of the mainmast.

For almost a minute, nothing happened.

Then the needles jiggled, leapt up from the deck, and began weaving through the sails.

A seagull peered down from the crow's nest, shook its head in disbelief, and flew off.

"The needles are haunted," Humphrey said, bumping the mast.

Only Tabitha Tumbly and myself knew the truth.

8
Ginger Pop

"How romantic!" Eleanor hummed. "The gentle rush of the ocean waves, the cry of gulls—"

She was interrupted by a tremendous din below deck.

"What's that noise?" I said, hiding behind Agatha's breezy hair.

"Pirate singing," Tabitha said.

The hatch opened, more slowly this time, and out floated the pirate with the wooden leg. He hiccuped, hit his head on the mainsail, and fell asleep.

"The pirates have been at the ginger pop," Charlie said, "and the bubbles have gone to their heads."

Several more pirates floated out, singing sea shanties and swaying this way and that.

"I hope the pirates don't see the haunted needles," I said.

Wither scratched his lightbulb head with a candle-like forefinger. "Tabitha, those needles aren't haunted at all. You're moving them yourself, using your poltergeist powers."

"You must think I'm a frightful show-off," Tabitha said, and she blushed.

"Not at all. It's just—I've had an idea, and—"

"The ropes!" Humphrey cried, and he gave the poet a bump.

"Yes," Wither said. "That was my idea. The ropes."

The pirates were so busy singing sea

shanties at the front of the ship—on the ship's bow, I mean—that they failed to see one of the ropes uncoil itself and slither across the deck.

When the rope reached the nearest of the pirates, a fat, hairy one with arms like tree trunks and a bristly mustache, it leapt from the planks like a snake and wound itself around the pirate's purple pantaloons.

The pirate hit the deck with a *THUMP*. Of course, the other pirates were too busy slapping their thighs to notice.

"Yo ho ho and a bottle of rum!" they sang. "Wither's poems are drivel and they're way too long!"

"What a mean song," said Wither.

The pirate in the purple pantaloons tried to wriggle free of the rope, but the more he tried to escape, the tighter the rope became.

"Serves him right for being mean," Wither said.

"Tabitha, try another," Charlie said. "That is, if you wouldn't mind."

Tabitha winked at another rope and sent it soaring through the salty air, where it bound the pirate with the wooden leg to the ship's mast.

One of the other pirates saw what had happened. "Ooh-arrr!" he cried angrily. "We can't 'ave that, you ghostly landlubbers!"

The rest of the pirates stopped singing and drew their cutlasses, baring their rotten teeth.

"Now we're in for it," Humphrey said as the pirates floated toward us. "They'll lock us in that sock trunk."

"Or leave us on a desert island, with one palm tree and an angry baboon," Wither said, his voice and fingers trembling.

"Not if Tabitha has anything to do with it," Charlie said. "Tabitha?"

We waited for Tabitha to waft into action, filling the air with ropes, but she just smiled shyly.

"Why have you stopped, Tabitha?" Eleanor said.

Tabitha bit her lip. "Um—"

"Elementary mathematics," Wither said, counting on his pencil-thin fingers. "There are more pirates than ropes."

"We'll just have to hope that we reach dry land," Charlie said, "before the pirates run out of ginger pop."

"The sails are still full of holes," Agatha said. "Until the sails are repaired, this ship can do nothing but drift."

"Then we're finished," Wither said, and he let out a loud, poetic blub.

9

The Ghost Ship

"We're sorry to trouble you," Charlie said as the phantom pirates closed in, "but would you mind taking us prisoner?"

"We've decided to give ourselves up," Wither said. He blew his nose and waved the white hanky above his head.

"No need to make us float the plank," I said.

"The plank?" the Captain said, ruffling his beard. "I hadn't thought of that."

Tooth Rot pointed his cutlass at Wither and steered the blubbing poet toward the plank.

"Not quite what I had in mind when I packed my trunks," Wither said.

"You next," the Captain boomed, and he wagged a finger at Charlie Vapor.

"Um, ladies first," Charlie said, being both polite and mean at the same time.

"Float, the lot of you!" the Captain yelled.

The stormy ocean terrified us, but we were afraid of the pirates, too, so we all floated to the far end of the plank, Wither reciting a farewell poem, Eleanor taking notes for her novel.

The odd thing was, when we ran out of plank, nothing happened.

"Curious," Wither said, and he scratched his forehead with a barnacle thumb.

"Thank heavens!" Agatha said. "Had we been still alive, we'd be dead."

"Well?" the Captain yelled. "What are you waiting for?"

"You're meant to plunge into the murky depths," Tooth Rot said.

"I don't think we could if we tried," Eleanor said.

Captain Mean-Beard frowned. "You might as well float back then. There's a mist descending, and I don't want you to catch cold."

As we flitted back along the plank, the phantom pirates again drew their cutlasses and bared their mean-spirited teeth.

"They can't jab us," Humphrey said as the mist swirled around his belly. "The phantom cutlasses will pass right through."

"I'm not so sure," Wither blubbed.

"Tooth Rot," the Captain boomed, "tie 'em up and lock 'em in the hold."

"That doesn't sound so bad," Agatha said. "At least we get to stay indoors till we reach dry land."

"I thought we were leaving them on a desert island," Tooth Rot said. "A small one, with one palm tree and an angry baboon."

The Captain laughed heartily and slapped his leather-clad thigh. "I'd forgotten about that."

We were about to beg for mercy when the mist cleared, and something far more chilling floated into view.

The phantom pirates dropped their cutlasses and turned a ghostly white.

A ghost ship!

And I don't mean a ship haunted by ghosties, like the *Raggy Dolly*. No, this was a ship so old that it existed only as a white wispy cloud.

"Ooh-arr!" the Captain cried, raising his telescope to his left eye patch. "What in heaven's name is that?"

"Saved!" Tabitha cried. "We can float aboard the ghost ship and hitch a ride home."

"That would be lovely," I said. "Only the ghost ship is flying a transparent skull and crossbones."

10
Boom!

The ghost ship sailed so close, I feared for a moment it would pass right through the *Raggy Dolly* and out the other side.

Its crew was more faded and wispy than the pirates who sailed the *Raggy Dolly*, but they were no less horrifying. They were dressed in elaborate Elizabethan costume, like our phantom friend Headless Leslie. Yet while Leslie had a cheerful face and a neatly trimmed beard, these Elizabethans looked as though they had spent several years lost at sea.

"Ooh-arr!" the Elizabethan pirates cried, drawing their cutlasses.

"Ooh-aarrr!" yelled the crew of the *Raggy Dolly*.

For several minutes, the two bands of merry pirates did nothing but stare across the short stretch of water, the waves crashing below.

"Captain, I think we'd better attack," Tooth Rot said, "or we'll be here all day."

"Peg Leg," Captain Mean-Beard said, "fire the cannon."

"How mean," Wither cooed, and we all stuck our fingers in our ears.

Peg Leg struck a match on his wooden leg and lit the fuse, and the cannonball shot out of the cannon with a terrifying *BOOM!*

The cannonball passed through the ghost ship and splashed into the sea.

"That old Elizabethan pirate ship is too

faded to be damaged by cannon fire," Charlie whispered, and he adjusted his fedora.

"That'll teach 'em," the Captain chuckled.

"I don't think it will," said the pirate with the hook hand. "They're lighting their own cannon. We'll be sunk!"

"Here we go again," Humphrey said, and we blocked our ears and bowed our heads.

I expected the whole ship to shake and sink to the bottom of the sea, taking seven frightfully friendly ghosties with it.

But the cannonball passed right through.

"Their wispy cannonballs are too faded to sink the *Raggy Dolly*," Charlie said, and he straightened his tie.

"They can't touch us!" the Captain roared.

"Yes," Tooth Rot said as gulls wheeled overhead. "And we can't touch them."

Captain Mean-Beard ruffled his mean beard.

"Safe to sail another day."

"Unless they decide to invade," Tooth Rot said.

At that moment, several dozen Elizabethan pirates flitted out from the ghost ship and wafted across the water.

The air filled with the clashing of cutlasses and cries of "Shiver me timbers!"

"We'd better hide," Tabitha said, her voice shaking. "But where?"

"Let's ask the expert," Charlie said, adjusting his cufflinks. "Pamela?"

"In here," I said, and we all wisped into a wooden barrel.

11

Fish Fingers

"Is that everyone?" Wither said. "It's too dark in here to tell."

"There should be seven pairs of eyes," Agatha said. "No one blink, and we'll take a count. Wither?"

"One, two, three," Wither counted, "four, five, six. And that large pair of eyes makes seven."

For a moment we listened nervously to the commotion outside, then Tabitha said, "Wither, did you say you counted seven pairs of eyes?"

"Fourteen eyeballs precisely," Wither said.

"If you counted seven pairs of eyes," Tabitha said, "unless you can see your reflection in a mirror, there must be eight of us."

I heard a scraping sound as Wither scratched his head with a thoughtful fingernail. "Hmm."

"Tabitha has a point," I said. "After all, you can see *with* your eyes, but you can't *see* your eyes, if you catch my drift."

"That being the case," Eleanor said, "us frightfully friendly ghosties are not alone."

"I'll light a match," Charlie said, and he did.

As the flickering orange light filled the barrel, we were greeted by the face of a young still-alive boy.

"Good afternoon," Charlie said, doffing his hat politely, but the boy said nothing.

"The poor chap looks frightened," Wither said.

"Don't be scared of us," I said. "We may be

ghosties, but we're frightfully friendly."

"Allow us to introduce ourselves," Charlie said. "I'm Charlie Vapor, and this is Pamela, Tabitha, Agatha, Eleanor, Humphrey, and Wither."

"Hello," the still-alive boy said quietly, and he smiled.

"How long have you been here?" Tabitha asked him.

"Since yesterday," the boy said.

"Ouch!" Charlie said, and he shook the match until it went out.

"You must be starved," Humphrey said in the dark.

"Not in the least," the boy said. "I had my packed lunch with me. Two ham rolls, a bar of chocolate, an apple, and a bag of cheese-and-onion chips."

"How did you find yourself curled up in a barrel on the deck of a pirate ship?" Agatha said

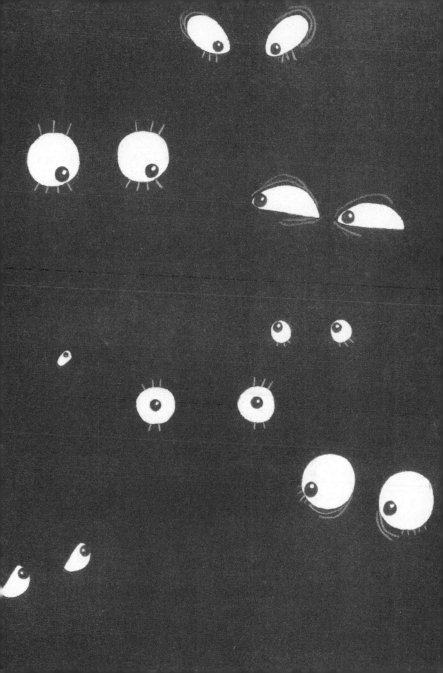

as Charlie struck another match.

"My parents were taking me on a summer cruise," the boy said. "We'd just boarded the ocean liner when I saw this creaky old ship. I wanted to explore, so I ran back down the gangplank and hopped aboard."

"Your mom and dad will be worried sick," Wither cooed.

"They won't miss me," the boy said. "My mom thinks I'm with my dad, and my dad thinks I'm with my mom. They don't talk to each other, you see."

"We'll get you back to that ocean liner," I said, "safe and sound."

"Not yet, though," Tabitha said. "We're in a spot of trouble ourselves."

"The ship is under attack from another band of pirates," Wither told the boy.

"And these chaps are even meaner than the

crew of the *Raggy Dolly*," Charlie added.

"I wondered what all the noise was," the boy said, and he frowned.

The second match went out. Charlie struck a third.

"Let's stay in here," Agatha said, "until the ship reaches dry land."

"We'll be quite safe if we keep our heads down," Tabitha said.

"Quite safe?" I said with a gulp. "How safe precisely?"

Charlie peered out through a knot in the wood. "It's safer to say we're in quite a lot of trouble."

Humphrey bumped him out of the way and put his eye to the hole. "The Elizabethan pirates have the *Raggy Dolly* crew surrounded."

"As long as they don't have *us* surrounded," Wither said.

"They haven't," Humphrey said, peering over the rim of the barrel. "Look, that one's eating fish fingers." He licked his lips and flitted out.

"That boy will put us all in danger," Charlie said.

"You'd better float out and fetch him," Tabitha said.

"I'm not floating out there," Charlie said. "There are pirates out there, and—"

Charlie's hat leapt from his head and floated onto the deck.

"Tabitha, you did that with your powers, so I'd have to retrieve it," Charlie said, handing Tabitha the box of matches.

"While you're out there," Agatha said as Charlie floated through the wood, "fetch Humphrey Bump."

A minute passed, and neither ghosty returned.

"Flit out after them, Wither," Tabitha said,

striking the last match.

"I'd rather not, Tabitha. Two frightfully friendly ghosties can waft unnoticed, but three would stick out like a sore thumb."

"Get on with it," Eleanor said, and out Wither wisped.

A minute later, Agatha said, "I suppose we'd better rescue them."

"All girls together!" Tabitha said. And she held hands with Agatha and Eleanor and led them out into the damp afternoon air.

That left me, Pamela Fraidy, alone in the barrel with the poor, frightened still-alive boy and an empty matchbox.

12

The Mermaid's Tale

Something had to be done. I didn't know what, but I knew I wouldn't find the answer in a barrel.

"We'll be back, I promise," I told the boy, and I flitted out through a knot in the wood.

One look at those Elizabethan pirates, however, and I lost my nerve and wisped over the wooden rail and down into the ocean.

You must think I'm frightfully brave. The truth is, I didn't feel brave at all.

I'd never been under the sea before. It was more green than blue, and it was wibbly and wafty, with hundreds of fish and plankton.

Bobbing floatily on the seabed, I felt oddly peaceful, and not afraid at all.

Then, I heard a voice.

"You look lost," the voice sang, and I turned to see the smiling face of a pretty young woman.

"Oh, I thought I was alone," I said. Then I noticed that the woman had a long, scaly tale. "Are you a mermaid?"

"I am," she sang. "Are you a ghost?"

"Yes," I said, and I blushed. "My name's Pamela Fraidy. Not that I'm afraid or anything."

I gazed up at the underside of the *Raggy Dolly* and explained how my friends and I were caught in a battle between two crews of phantom pirates.

"I found myself in a tight spot myself once," the mermaid sang.

"How frightful."

"There I was, swimming through the seaweed,

when a treasure chest slammed shut and caught the tip of my tail."

"That must've hurt."

"Not in the least, but I couldn't swim away."

"And you needed to swim to the surface for air?"

"No," the mermaid sang. "I breathe through my gills. It's just that I like to read magazines, and I wanted to buy the latest issue of *Deep Sea Life*."

"What did you do?"

"One thing I have learned during my time as an enchanted creature," the mermaid sang, "is that there are times when the problem is the solution."

"I don't understand," I said, and I rolled my eyes.

The mermaid rolled her eyes. "Consider the object that trapped me."

"A treasure chest!"

"I needed a passer-by to open the chest," the mermaid explained in song, "and if there is one thing a passer-by is sure to open, it is a chest laden with treasure."

"How true!"

"The problem was, the treasure chest lay hidden among the seaweed."

"What did you do?"

"I wafted the seaweed away with my arm, revealing the decorative chest. A moment later, a passing sea urchin opened the chest and nabbed the sparkly treasure."

"I don't know what a sea urchin is," I said, "but I'm glad the sea urchin helped you."

"Like I told you," the mermaid sang, "there are times when the problem is the solution."

The moment I heard these bubbly words, I knew how my friends and I would rescue the still-alive boy from the *Raggy Dolly*.

"It's been lovely talking to you," I said, and I waved good-bye to the mermaid and floated up through the wobbly water.

13

Pamela's Plan

The problem was, when I floated up over the railings, my frightfully friendly friends were nowhere to be seen.

"Oh dear," I said as one of the Elizabethan pirates tried to jab me.

Just then, Charlie wafted by. "This way," he said politely, taking me by the hand. "That is, if you don't mind."

"Not in the least," I said. "I enjoy being rescued, particularly when in grave danger."

Charlie led me over the heads and beneath

the wafty legs of pirates locked in swashbuckling combat, to where Tabitha, Agatha, Eleanor, Humphrey, and Wither cowered at the ship's bow.

"We have to get that still-alive boy out of that barrel," Tabitha said, "but where will we take him?"

"I have an idea," I said. "Well, just a thought, really. Sometimes, um—"

"Get on with it," Wither said.

"I've forgotten what it was now."

We heard a loud "Ooh-arrr!" as Captain Mean-Beard wisped toward us from the ship's portside.

"It seems to me," I said, thinking back to the mermaid's tale, "that sometimes the problem is the solution."

Wither folded his mast-like arms. "I fail to see how pirates can solve the problem of pirates."

"That's not what I meant. If the Elizabethan pirates have all boarded the *Raggy Dolly*, the ghost ship will be deserted. We can sail the wispy ghost ship all the way home!"

"Pamela Fraidy," Charlie said, "that is the cleverest plan I have heard all day."

"I'm not so sure," Eleanor said. "That ship is so wispy, the still-alive boy will pass through the deck and fall into the sea."

"We'll just have to carry him," Tabitha said.

"Like I said," Charlie went on, "it's a terrific plan. If it doesn't work, I'll eat my fedora."

"Let's get a move on," Humphrey said, "before the Captain jabs us with his cutlass."

"Still-alive boy?" Wither said as we wisped into the barrel. "Are you still here?"

"Yes," a voice said in the dark. "Are you going to rescue me?"

"If you promise to trust us and hold on tight," Eleanor said, and we wisped the boy high into the air.

"Oh!" the boy cried. "How tiny the ship looks

from up here."

"I wouldn't know," I said
with my eyes closed.

"It's funny," the boy said,
"but I don't feel afraid at all.
Though I'd like to know
where you're taking me."

"Sometimes," Agatha said,
"the solution is the problem.
Or is it the other way around?"

"We're going to board the
Elizabethan pirate ship,"
Tabitha told the boy, "and
sail it all the way home."

"Wait," the boy said.
"There's—"

"We're well aware that the ghost ship is
wispy," Wither told him. "You'll be fine if you
hold on tight."

"That wasn't what I meant."

"It's not always true that ghosts pass through things, or that things always pass through ghosts," Tabitha said. "That's just in storybooks and cartoons."

"The only ghosty who can always pass through," Agatha said, "day in, day out, rain or shine, is dear Charlie Vapor."

Charlie doffed his hat, the polite thing to do, even when fleeing swashbuckling pirates.

It was Charlie who led the way. "Left a bit," he'd say, enjoying himself immensely. "Right a bit. Mind that seagull! That's it, now wisp down."

"Stop!" the still-alive boy said. "There's something—"

"Don't you worry an ounce," Wither said as we floated toward the wispy deck. "Hold on tight, and all will be well."

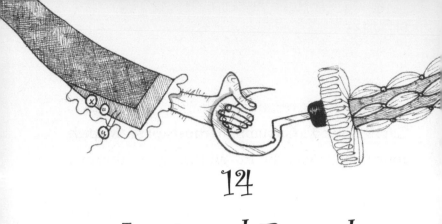

14

Lost and Found

The ghost ship was eerily silent. No creaking of wood, no rustling of sails, no cry of gulls. Even the crash of the waves below sounded muffled.

"We'd better float into the cabin," Tabitha said, "or the pirates on the deck of the *Raggy Dolly* will see us."

The moment Agatha's hand touched the door handle, the door evaporated, only to materialize further along the wispy wooden wall.

"You'd better hurry, Aggie dear," Eleanor said. "I think the phantom pirates may have seen us."

Across the water, we could see the Elizabethan Captain and Captain Mean-Beard wisping above the bow of the *Raggy Dolly*.

"This," Wither said, "will be a battle to behold."

But rather than fight, the two phantom Captains tossed their cutlasses onto the deck, slapped each other heartily on the back and shook hands.

"How frightfully friendly," I said.

"If the pirates are joining forces," Charlie said, "they won't be needing their old ghost ship."

"In that case," Tabitha said, "they won't mind if we steer it all the way to England."

"Wait!" the still-alive boy said. "I have something to tell you."

"We'd better listen to the lad," Charlie said, adjusting his cufflinks.

"Remember when you counted seven pairs of eyeballs?" the boy said. "When you lifted me from the barrel, I could count only six."

"Plus your own wondrous orbs," Wither said. "Six plus one equals seven."

"Wither, the boy is right," Agatha said. "There should be eight pairs of eyeballs, not seven."

"Which of us is missing?" Tabitha said.

"Let's ask Humphrey," Wither said. "The Bump boy is good with this sort of thing. Humphrey, which . . . ?" Wither scratched his seagull head with a claw-like finger. "I say, where's Humphrey?"

We were about to start calling Humphrey's name when Humphrey came tumbling toward us through the air.

"Humphrey," Tabitha said, "where have you been?"

"I found the pirates' secret stash of fish fingers. I had to eat them before they went off."

"Well, you've arrived just in time," I said. "We're about to set sail for England."

"I think we'd better sail in the opposite direction," Humphrey said. "I heard the pirates talking. They plan to invade the ocean liner the *Porcelain Princess*."

"Ooh, how mean," Wither said, and he pursed his lips.

"I knew those ghostly pirates were up to no good," Charlie said.

"First thing's first," Tabitha said. "The phantom pirates are flitting across the water. If we hide in the cabin, they might forget we're here and wisp away."

"The door handle keeps evaporating," Agatha said, grasping desperately.

"There's nothing else for it," Charlie said. "We'll have to pass through the wall."

"That's easy for you to say," I said. "You're the only ghosty who can pass through, Charlie."

"I'd bet any ghosty can pass through a wall as

wispy as that," Charlie said.

"I must say," Agatha said, "I do find the thought unnerving."

"You can do it," Charlie said, holding his fedora to his chest. "I pass through solid walls all the time, and this wall is as light and wispy as cloud."

"Charlie is right," Eleanor said. "Even a still-alive could pass through a wall so wispy."

Charlie passed through first, followed by Wither, then Humphrey, with the still-alive boy sat on his shoulders.

"All girls together!" Tabitha said, and she took my hand and Agatha's hand, and Agatha held hands with Eleanor Wraith, and a moment later we found ourselves on the other side of the wispy wall.

15

Dressing Up

"With so many pirates searching for us," Agatha said, peering out through the cabin window, "wherever we hide, they're sure to find us."

"Hmm," Wither said, and he made that face like he's chewing a wasp. "What if we dress up as pirates ourselves? This wispy ship is so laden with junk, there's sure to be pirate clothing somewhere."

"There's a coat stand behind the door," Eleanor said, "and this wispy wicker basket is stuffed full of pirate hats."

Before you could say "shipshape," us seven

frightfully friendly ghosties were dressed from head to transparent bits as mean-spirited, swashbuckling pirates. Ooh-arrr!

"What about me?" the still-alive boy said. "I can't wear a ghostly pirate outfit. And if I don't dress as a pirate, the real ghost pirates will recognize me, and they'll make me walk the plank."

"Not if we have anything to do with it," I said, sounding quite brave, I thought.

But then the wall parted like a phantom curtain, and I lost my nerve and hid behind Wither's eye patch.

"Ooh-arrr!" the pirates cried as I peered out. There were an awful lot of them—pirates from Captain Mean-Beard's crew and Elizabethan pirates in those lovely old-fashioned costumes, all baring their teeth.

Charlie doffed his pirate hat. "Yo ho ho," he said politely. "And, um, a bottle of fizzy ginger pop."

"You lot are stowaways," one of the Elizabethan pirates growled.

"Actually, we're not," Tabitha said.

"We're pirates, like you 'orrible lot," Humphrey said, and he gave the pirate a bump.

"And this still-alive boy is our prisoner," Agatha said.

"If you're pirates," one of Captain Mean-Beard's crew said, "sing us a sea shanty, to prove it."

"I know a terrific sea shanty," Eleanor whispered. "I read about sea shanties while researching for my second novel, *The Wave Doth Tumble*."

"Oh, what a poignant title!" Wither crooned, and I wisped out from behind the eye patch as his eyes filled with tears.

"Away, ho, away!" Eleanor sang. "Away, away, ahoy!"

One of the Elizabethan pirates rubbed his crooked nose with his hook hand. "Is that it?"

"I'll sing it again if you like," Eleanor said.

The pirates were just drawing their cutlasses when the wardrobe door creaked open and out tumbled a ghostly white parrot.

"Ooh-arr!" the pirates cried as the parrot flapped around the cabin.

The funny thing was, the parrot took a shine to Wither.

"Get off me!" Wither cried as the bird perched on the top of his pirate hat. "I'm allergic to feathers. *AAA-CHOOOO!*"

"Let's leave 'em to it," one of the Elizabethan pirates growled. "If these crazy ghosties aren't pirates, I'll eat my pirate hat."

16
Force-Ten Gale

We watched through the cabin window as the pirates wisped high over the waves, back to the *Raggy Dolly*.

"We're not out of trouble yet," Wither said. "There's a gale blowing in. And if we don't reach the *Porcelain Princess* before those mean-spirited pirates, the holler-days of thousands of still-alive families will be ruined."

"My mom and dad are on that ocean liner," the still-alive boy said.

"Look!" Agatha said, peering out through the

cabin's wispy window. "The *Raggy Dolly* has set sail."

"And in this wind it's sure to move at a terrific pace," Tabitha said.

"If this storm is so fierce," Wither said as the phantom parrot pecked his nose, "why are we not moving?"

"You have to stow the anchor," the boy said. "We learned about sailing ships at school."

We flitted around the ship until we found the ghostly wooden winch. As we turned the haunted handle, the wispy rope grew thinner and thinner, then faded into nothing.

"This ghost ship is so old," Agatha said once we had gathered on the top deck, "it has started to evaporate."

"Now we know why the Elizabethan pirates were so keen to commandeer the *Raggy Dolly*," Tabitha said.

"We must reach the ocean liner before we run out of boat," Wither said, the wind howling through his ears. "Quite how we go about it, I have no idea."

"Hoist the mainsail!" Humphrey said as the still-alive boy clung to his shoulders. "And, um, do something with the rigging!"

We did just that.

Fortunately the ghost ship was lighter than the *Raggy Dolly*, so we soon caught up with the pirates.

"Ahoy there!" we called as our floaty boat wisped past, the sails billowing like Wither's long johns on the clothes line.

90

The storm grew fierce, and it wasn't long before the ocean liner appeared on the horizon.

"There she blows!" Charlie cried, holding on to his pirate hat. "The *Porcelain Princess*, in all her glory."

"Let's hope we reach it," Tabitha said, "while our ghost ship is still ship-shaped."

17

The Porcelain Princess

As we dropped anchor, the still-alive passengers ran into their cabins, waving their arms above their heads.

"They're waving at us, to say hello," Tabitha said.

"It is the polite thing to do," Charlie said, doffing his pirate hat.

"If the still-alives are so happy to see us," I said, a little shyly, "why have they gone inside?"

"They'll be out again in a moment," Tabitha said. "I expect they're combing their hair or putting on their best clothes."

We waited in the blustery breeze for a minute or so, but the still-alives remained in their cabins.

"Perhaps someone warned the holler-day makers about the pirates," Agatha said.

"No, that's not it," the still-alive boy said. "People who are still alive find ghosts frightening. The passengers ran into their cabins to hide."

"How mean!" Wither said as the parrot flapped its wings.

"I don't know why they'd be afraid of us," I said. "We're frightfully friendly."

While we floated around the ghost ship, trying to decide what to do, we barely noticed the *Raggy Dolly* drop anchor alongside the *Porcelain Princess*. The pirates drew their cutlasses and wisped across the tumbling waves.

"Oh dear," Wither said, plucking ghostly feathers from his pirate blouse. "What are we to do?"

"It's too late to warn the passengers now,"

Agatha said.

If the still-alives were afraid of us friendly ghosties, the sight of the phantom pirates terrified them.

"Help!" the still-alive passengers cried. "Help!"

We heard a *SPLOSH*, then another and another, as lifeboats hit the surface of the water.

"The still-alives are trying to escape," Agatha said.

The pirates flitted down from the ocean liner's deck and wisped around the lifeboats.

"And now the pirates are rounding them up," Tabitha said.

"Does their meanness know no bounds?" Wither said, and he sneezed.

By now, our ghost ship resembled little more than a blob of cloud.

"We'd better float aboard," Tabitha said, "before it's too late."

"The phantoms won't harm us," Charlie said. "Not while we're disguised as pirates."

Humphrey lifted the still-alive boy onto his shoulders and we wafted over to the deck of the *Porcelain Princess*. When we looked back, our ghost ship had vanished.

"What are you doing with that still-alive boy?" one of the Elizabethan pirates growled.

Tabitha shrugged. "Um . . ."

"All prisoners are to be kept below deck," the pirate yelled, his earrings jangling in the breeze.

"That," Wither said, "is precisely where we intend to take him. *AAA-CHOOOO!*"

18

Cabins and Corridors

"What a beautiful boat," Wither whispered as we floated below deck, the parrot pecking his left ear.

"Look at that lampshade," Agatha hummed, gazing up at the ceiling. "Like hundreds of glass tears."

"It's a chandelier," Eleanor whispered back. "I have one just like it in my downstairs loo."

"This is no time to be admiring the decor," I whispered. "We have to rescue the still-alives."

"Yes, and fast," Eleanor whispered, scrawling

in her notebook. "I've never seen so many unhappy faces."

"I'm not surprised that the still-alives are unhappy," Tabitha whispered. "One minute you're enjoying a summer holler-day, the next a bunch of phantom pirates poke you with their cutlasses and order you into the dining saloon."

We waited till the pirates had wisped up to the top deck, then lowered the still-alive boy to his feet. "It's nice to be able to walk again," the boy said. "On fancy carpet too."

Of course, the still-alives thought we were real pirates. "Don't worry," the boy would tell them as we passed. "These ghosts are my friends."

"We're not actually pirates at all," Charlie would say, and he'd doff his pirate hat and wink.

"Ghosties we may be," Wither would add, "but we're frightfully friendly."

We stopped by a grand piano with a

sophisticated old lady cowering beneath it. "Excuse me, madam," Charlie said, "but could you tell us where we might find the ship's Captain?"

"They're—they're holding the poor chap p-prisoner in a broom closet," the old lady stammered. "Follow that corridor, and turn left at the painting of the *Titanic*."

We passed a dozen doors before we found one with a gold sign reading BROOM CLOSET. The still-alive boy tried to open the door, but it was locked.

"The poor man looks frightened out of his wits," Tabitha said, peering through the keyhole. "Pass through, Charlie. Tell him we're here to help."

Charlie Vapor doffed his hat—the polite thing to do—and passed through the door.

The rest of us put our ears to the wood.

"Please do forgive the intrusion," we heard

Charlie say. "The fact is, I'm not a pirate at all."

"Aargh!" the Captain screamed. "Keep away from me, spirit!"

"A ghosty I may be," Charlie said, "but I'm frightfully friendly."

"These ghosts are my friends," the still-alive boy yelled through the keyhole. "They rescued me from the pirate ship, and they're here to rescue you and every passenger on this ocean liner."

"I have to admit," the Captain said to Charlie, "you're too polite to be a pirate. You'll find a spare key on the hook by the painting of the *Titanic*."

The still-alive boy ran back to the painting and lifted the key from the hook.

A moment later, the ship's Captain, a round man with a neat orange beard, stood blinking in the open doorway. "I hope you have a plan," he said, straightening his cap.

"I'm not sure that we do," Tabitha said.

19

Garlic Wafts

Wither wrinkled his nose. "What's that wafty smell? It's coming from the other side of this air vent."

The Captain led us down the corridor to a door with a sign reading CARGO.

"Garlic," the Captain said, opening the door. "Tonight was to be the night of the *Porcelain Princess*'s Annual Garlic Festival. These ten crates are packed with fresh garlic bulbs."

The seven of us ghosties held our noses. GARLIC, read the words painted on the crates. HANDLE WITH CARE.

"If you think it smells now," the Captain said, "you wait till we unpack it."

"Ghosties hate garlic," Tabitha explained.

The Captain shrugged. "Garlic is said to ward off evil spirits."

"It wards off friendly spirits too," Agatha said.

A man in a checked suit came racing down the corridor, holding a leather case in his left hand. He squeezed past the Captain's tummy and sprinted off toward a stairwell.

"Who's that man?" the boy asked.

"Him? That's Harold Unwhiff, the nose-plug salesman," the Captain said. "Mr. Unwhiff is a millionaire. I expect he bribed the pirates to let him go free, and he's running away before they change their mind."

"If that man is a nose-plug salesman," Charlie said, adjusting his cufflinks, "that case will be full of nose plugs."

Harold Unwhiff was about to disappear up the stairs when we heard the loudest *SPLASH* you could ever imagine.

"What in the name of my auntie's bloomers was that?" Harold said, backing away from the stairs.

"Only one thing on this ocean liner could make a splash as loud as that," the Captain said. "The engine!"

The Captain led us ghosties and the still-alive boy down several corridors to a door with a sign reading ENGINE ROOM.

"Oh my!" the Captain cried as he opened the door. "Those phantom pirates have hauled out the engine and pushed it overboard."

"Why would they do that?" I said.

"The pirates want to turn this ocean liner into a floating pirate hotel," Humphrey said. "I heard them talking about it."

"We need a plan," Tabitha said.

Wither rubbed his chin. "Let's see. We're trapped on an ocean liner with ten crates of garlic and a case of sample nose plugs. Hmm."

"Well?" the Captain said impatiently. "Any ideas?"

"The answer is obvious," Wither said. "We feed the garlic to the seagulls, then write HELP on the nose plugs and fling them into the sea."

"Wither, that's a terrible idea," Charlie said. "Do you have any ideas, Pamela?"

"Only one," I said shyly. "We could use the garlic to frighten away the phantom pirates. If we block our nostrils with the nose plugs, the garlic won't affect us."

"Another clever plan from Pamela Fraidy!" Charlie said, and he doffed his hat.

I was about to point out that the plan would only work if we could find Harold Unwhiff, when Harold came running down the corridor, quite out of breath.

"Ah, just the man," the Captain said. "Harold, we need your help."

"Can't stop!" Harold said between puffs. "I'm running from the phantom pirates."

As the salesman turned a corner, his briefcase popped open and several nose plugs rolled onto the carpet.

"You don't need to run from these phantoms," the Captain told the salesman. "The pirate outfits are a disguise."

"They're frightfully friendly," the boy said, and he laughed.

"After what I've seen today," Harold said, picking up the nose plugs, "that doesn't surprise me in the least."

106

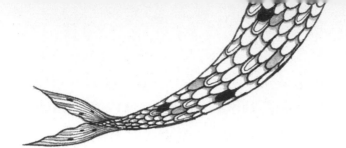

20

The Mermaid's Tail

"Harold," the Captain said as we took off our pirate costumes, "hand me those nose plugs."

"They're not for sale," Harold said. "These are just samples."

"You'll get them back," Tabitha said. "We just want to borrow them while we frighten away the phantom pirates."

"If they'll help you get rid of those scallywags," Harold said, "you can keep them."

We each chose a pair of nose plugs and fitted them into our ghosty nostrils.

"Captain," Tabitha said, "what's the quickest way back to the crates of garlic?"

"This way," the Captain said, and he led the still-alive boy and us seven ghosties straight to the door labeled CARGO.

"I can barely smell the garlic at all," Agatha said as the Captain pried open the first crate.

Harold smiled proudly. "I only sell the best," he said. "Those are the finest nose plugs in the world."

The next part of the plan was to hang garlic bulbs all over the ship, but we couldn't do that on our own. We needed the still-alives to help.

Passing the garlic bulbs around the ocean liner was easier than you might think. The moment a still-alive hung a bulb around their neck, the phantom pirates left them alone. The still-alive could then hand garlic bulbs to their family and friends.

"Here," Tabitha said, tucking a garlic clove into a vicar's collar. "Garlic, to ward off the phantom pirates."

"There's another nine crates of the stuff in the hold," Charlie said, handing a garlic clove to a chef. "Grab yourself a handful and pass them around."

A still-alive circus troupe strung garlic bulbs on a length of string and hung it along the corridors. Smiling children filled their pockets with garlic bulbs and stuck peeled cloves to cabin doors.

By now, the garlic fumes wafting around the corridors were so strong, even the still-alives had to hold their noses.

The phantom pirates did not like the smell one bit. "Ooh-arrr, me wafties!" they cried as they flitted out through the boat's portholes. "Back to the *Raggy Dolly*! Abandon ship!"

Soon, there wasn't a jangly hoop earring or a wooden leg in sight. As the news of the fleeing pirates spread up and down the corridors and stairwells, the still-alives began to shout and cheer.

"We did it!" the still-alives cried. "The pirates have left us alone!"

At that moment, a man and a woman stepped out of the crowd. "Timmy?"

The still-alive boy turned and smiled a broad, beaming smile. "Mom! Dad! And you're together!"

"We don't argue anymore," the boy's mother said, kissing him on the forehead. "This trip was just what we needed."

"I'd like you to meet my new friends," the still-alive boy said. "These friendly ghosts have saved the day!"

"I'm afraid we're not home and dry yet," Eleanor said, scrawling in her notebook. "This boat has no engine."

"The still-alives could escape in lifeboats," Humphrey said.

The Captain frowned. "There are five thousand vacationers on board the *Porcelain Princess*, and we're hundreds of miles from dry land."

"Perhaps my friend can help," I said, a little shyly. And I told Tabitha and the others about the mermaid I'd met at the bottom of the ocean.

"I've spent thirty years at sea," the Captain said, "and I've never believed in mermaids, giant squid, or any other fantastical sea creature. But then, until today, I didn't believe in spirits either."

"Whether this mermaid could help or not," Tabitha said as the Captain led us onto the deck, "she won't be able to do a thing if we can't find her."

The Captain leaned on the rail and breathed in the salty sea air. The storm had blown itself out and the sun was setting in the west. If we squinted our eyes, we could see the *Raggy Dolly* sailing over the horizon.

It was then that I began to lose hope.

"We'll never find my mermaid friend under

all those waves," I said, gazing out at the vast blue yonder.

The sun had almost set now, and the waves glistened in the light from the ocean liner's cabin windows.

"I'd radio for help," the Captain said, "but the pirates stole the ship's radio equipment."

"We're trapped!" Wither wailed poetically. "Left to drift forever on an ocean liner with no means of propulsion."

I was about to ask Wither what he was talking about when the still-alive boy leapt up and down excitedly. "Shh!" the boy said. "I can hear singing."

We listened.

At first we heard only the crash and tumble of waves. Then an enchanting voice floated up from the water. Peering over the rail, we saw an elegant figure bobbing among the foam.

The mermaid!

"There I was," the mermaid sang brightly, "flicking through the latest issue of *Deep Sea Life*, when a huge mechanical object plunged into the water. I wondered what it was at first, but then I glanced up and saw the underside of the *Porcelain Princess*."

"What a pretty mermaid," Eleanor said, scrawling notes in her notepad.

"Pretty she may be," the boy's father said, "but how can she help?"

"Leave this to me," I said, and I wisped over the rail and down to the surface of the water, leaving the other ghosties to marvel at my bravery.

"Hello, Pamela!" the mermaid sang as she combed her hair.

"The engine was tossed overboard by the phantom pirates," I explained. "They wanted to turn the ocean liner into a floating pirate hotel. Can you help us get home?"

"Certainly!" the mermaid sang. "My friends and I will tow the *Porcelain Princess* all the way to England."

The mermaid swished her tail, slapping it against the water, and hundreds of mermaids and mermen emerged from the foamy waves.

"Hooray!" the still-alives cried as they gazed down from the top deck. "Hooray for the mermaid!"

"And hooray for Pamela Fraidy!" the ghosties cheered as I floated back up.

"Pamela Bravery, don't you mean?" I said, and I smiled—just a *little* shyly.

That night, the still-alives threw a party on the top deck with dancing and colored lanterns and a brass band playing seaside songs, as our enchanted friends towed the *Porcelain Princess* all the way home.

Introducing
the ghosties in
Book 1
of the spookiest
series around!

*You still-alives are so
mean to us ghosties!*

Tabitha Tumbly, Charlie Vapor,
and friends can't understand
why the still-alives in their
house are so horrid.

When a still-alive locks
Pamela Fraidy in the attic, the
ghosties are determined to
make friends with them.

But will the still-alives accept
their ghosty friendship?

The ghosties go
on holler-day in
Book 2

*What better than
a ghostly holler-
day by the sea?*

But how are the
ghosties to decide
between Frighten-
on-Sea and
Scare-borough?

A postcard from their friend
Headless Leslie decides for them:
Headless is in Frighten and cannot
remember how to get home!

So the friends set off on an
exciting ghosty caper involving a
haunted pier, a funfair and a
spooky phantom magician . . .

Humphrey Bump
is causing trouble
at school in
Book 3

*What's more horrid
than a ghost school?*

Still-alive school,
of course!

Bumping is Humphrey Bump's favorite
thing, but when he is kicked out of
ghost school for dangerous bouncing,
he has to go to still-alive school!

The other ghosties are on hand to cause
a stir in the classroom, but this just
takes things from bad to worse . . .

Will Humphrey fight the bullies and triumph?

Find out in this feast of bouncy, ghosty fun!

For more spooky stories
and terrific tales visit:

www.quercus.com

@quercususa